In the same series:

Diogenes' Lantern
Prince Orpheus

Original French edition
© 2001 Desclée de Brouwer, Paris
English translation
© 2003 J. Paul Getty Trust

First published in English in the
United States of America in 2003 by
Getty Publications
1200 Getty Center Drive, Suite 500
Los Angeles, California 90049-1682
www.getty.edu

AT GETTY PUBLICATIONS:
Christopher Hudson, *Publisher*
Mark Greenberg, *Editor in Chief*
Ann Lucke, *Managing Editor*
Sharon Grevet, *Translator*

AT DESCLÉE DE BROUWER:
Claude Helft, *Managing Editor*
Mireille Cohedali, *Layout*
Yves Raffner, *Production*

Printed and bound in France
by Le Govic

Library of Congress
Cataloging-in-Publication Data

Klein-Gousseff, Catherine.
  [Le chevalier parfait. English]
  The perfect knight / Catherine
Gousseff ; illustrated by Fabian
Negrin.
       p. cm.
Summary: When a damsel asks a
knight what he did to make himself
perfect, she discovers that he has
made war and tells him that he is,
therefore, not as perfect as she
believed.
  ISBN 0-89236-739-3
  [1. Knights and knighthood—
Fiction. 2. Peace—Fiction.
3. Behavior—Fiction. 4. Middle
Ages—Fiction.] I. Negrin, Fabian,
ill. II. Title.
  PZ7.K6783535Pe 2004
  [Fic]—dc22
                    2003012148

Catherine Gousseff

The Perfect Knight

Illustrated by Fabian Negrin

The J. Paul Getty Museum
Los Angeles

"Little knight, what was the first thing you did to make yourself perfect?"

"Beautiful damsel, I first learned to ride a horse bigger than me. Fearless, I galloped, I burst through the forest in winter and summer, through rain and wind, even when there were frightful bandits and plunderers.

"My dogs led me deep into the woods. At bears, deer, and boars I took aim with my bow. On my shoulder my tame hawk perched just so."

"Little knight, what was the next thing you did to make yourself perfect?"

"Beautiful damsel, one fine day, with no regrets, I left my parents and ran far away. Where did I go? To the lord in his castle. I became his page, both day and night. Sunrise to sunset, I served him alone. I polished his armor until it shone. I brought him his clothes and made sure they fit right. I took care of his horses. He taught me to fight. He took me along on his grand processions. He gave me his goodness, his greatest possession, and was like a father to me."

"Little knight, what did you do after that to make yourself perfect?"

"Beautiful damsel, I took an oath. I swore to help children, the weak, and the poor. I promised to remain my lord's friend evermore — for better or worse. They rang all the bells on the village square. O, the lords and ladies! You should have been there! On my knees I received from the hands of my lord a helmet, a shield, and a magnificent sword! Thus, I became a knight."

"Little knight, what more did you do
to make yourself perfect?"

"Beautiful damsel, on the land I was given
I built something greater than merely a
house: a castle surrounded by a moat, with
four strong towers—north, south, west,
and east. And then I invited all of my
friends to a sumptuous feast. O how we
dined. I served them my favorite courses;
there was delicious roast goose, fine
bottles of wine. While jugglers threw balls
high up into the sky, the troubadours
sang to the sound of a viol, telling tales
of knightly adventures so bold."

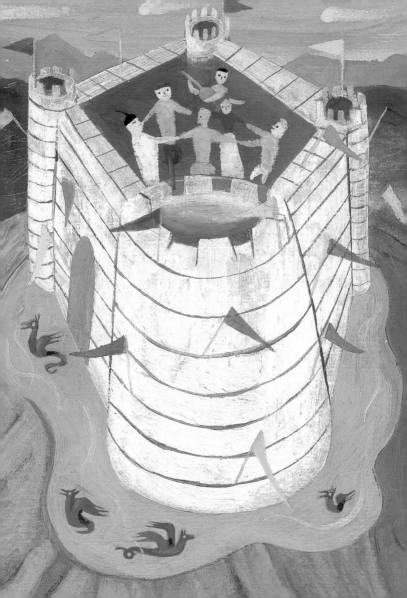

"Little knight, what else did you do to
  make yourself perfect?"

"Beautiful damsel, I found a lady who
  was all I could wish for. I loved her and
  asked her for only one thing: to look
  upon her while in her garden she strolled.
  I wrote poems in praise of her beauty,
  a sight to behold. I brought her musicians
  from faraway lands. Beneath her high
  window they played gorgeous music, with
  their flutes and their drums—what a
  heavenly band. My lady was coy, with eyes
  both modest and fair! She gave me three
  ribbons, which I tied to my sword with
  great care."

"Little knight, what did you do then to make
yourself perfect?"

"Beautiful damsel, carrying my banner and
wearing my finest armor, I went off to
a tournament to joust—my most favorite
sport. There, in front of the crowd, stood
Clotaire, the greatest of enemies. Pointing
my lance, I galloped straight at him; twenty-
one times he fell from his horse! Three
of his teeth were knocked out as he tumbled,
but twenty-one times he got up, didn't
crumble. (Once he nearly knocked *me*
off my horse.) For the very last time I took
careful aim. Off he fell! I won the fight!
The lords and ladies did exclaim, 'Hurrah,
hurrah for the little knight!'"

"Little knight, what was the last thing
you did to make yourself perfect?"

"Beautiful damsel, one day in spring, my
lord called on me to join him in war.
At once we departed for battle. We
burned many villages, left many peasants
in tatters. In a meadow we spied enemy
soldiers, a hundred strong, coming at
us like wolves! In the course of the battle
I lost my lance but not my sword:
many enemies died as I thrust it forward.
Flags flying, we returned to the castle,
our prisoners in tow."

"Little knight, if you have made war—
   if you burned, if you pillaged and killed
   and caused men to fall—then you're
   not perfect, not perfect at all."

"Beautiful damsel, then I give up: what
   does it take to be perfect?"

"What does it take? Why, the very
   opposite…"

"The opposite, beautiful damsel? And
   what, pray tell, is the opposite of war?"

"It is peace, my dear little knight.
   It is peace."